EAST RENFREWSHIRE

09~~~~7632

MR. MEN
ADVENTURE WITH
Knights

Original concept by
Roger Hargreaves

Written and illustrated by
Adam Hargreaves

EGMONT

Mr Uppity was very excited.

He was going to visit a friend.

A very important friend.

A friend who was a knight.

A knight called Sir Lance who lived in a castle,
to which he had invited many people for his annual
tournament, which was to be held the next day.

Just as Mr Uppity was driving his car over the moat, the drawbridge began to rise.

"Stop!" shrieked Mr Uppity.

But 'stop' was not going to stop anything because it was Mr Muddle who was operating the drawbridge.

If Mr Uppity had shouted, "Go!" then all might have been well, but he didn't.

Poor Mr Uppity.

It was not a good start to his visit.

There was a roaring log fire in the banqueting hall and Mr Uppity soon dried off.

Sir Lance had laid on a whole feast that evening and Mr Uppity and his friends ate very well indeed as they listened to the minstrel singing songs and telling tales.

Late that night, after everybody had gone to bed,
Little Miss Greedy woke up.

I'm sure you can guess why she woke up.

That's right, she was hungry!

So she set off to find the kitchen to get herself
a midnight snack.

The castle was a maze of turrets and battlements and
passageways and spiral staircases and in no time at
all Little Miss Greedy was hopelessly lost.

She kept going down and down.

Down and down until she found herself in the castle dungeon.

It was dark and damp and very creepy.

Little Miss Greedy gulped.

And then with a bang the door swung shut and Little Miss Greedy was locked in for the night!

It was a very cold and hungry Little Miss Greedy who was found by a knight the following morning.

And, it would have to be said, a very happy Little Miss Greedy when she found out it was time for breakfast!

Once everybody had eaten breakfast, Sir Lance showed them to the armoury where they got dressed for the tournament.

Mr Nosey could not find a helmet that fitted.

And nor could Mr Small.

Finding a helmet to fit Mr Skinny was not a problem, but it was too heavy.

Mr Fussy refused to wear one because it would mess up his hair.

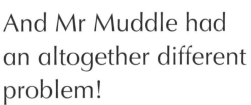

And Mr Muddle had an altogether different problem!

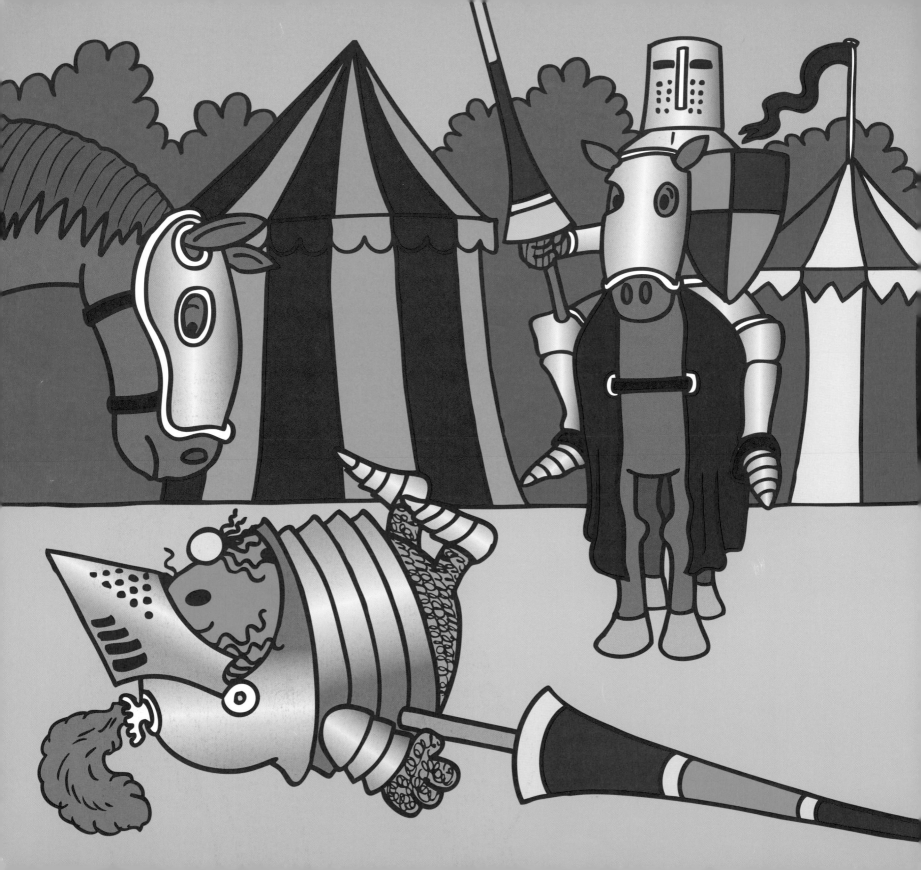

The tournament began with the jousting contest.

Mr Clumsy was the first to test his skills against
Sir Lance's knights.

But it will come as no surprise to hear
that Mr Clumsy was hopeless.

He kept falling off his horse before
he even got to the jousting yard.

"This is too easy!" cried Sir Lance.
"Is there nobody who can give
my knights a true test?"

"I'll have a go," said Mr Strong.

"You had better put your armour on," suggested Sir Lance.

"No need," replied Mr Strong.

And he was right.

He was so strong that the Green Knight's lance just bounced off him and he won the contest with ease.

The next challenge was sword fighting.

Sir Lance's knights all refused to fight Mr Strong,
so Mr Tickle stepped in.

He did not even need a sword to defeat the Red Knight.

The sword fighting was followed by the archery contest.

Mr Tickle's arms were altogether too long for archery.

So Little Miss Lucky decided to have a go, even though she had never shot a bow and arrow before.

She hit a bullseye first time.

"Beginner's luck!" exclaimed Sir Lance.

Little Miss Lucky hit the bullseye with her second arrow.

"I don't believe it!" cried Sir Lance.

And then Little Miss Lucky hit a third bullseye.

"Nobody's that lucky," grumbled Sir Lance.

"I am!" grinned Little Miss Lucky.

Just then a messenger ran through the crowd.

"Dragon!" he cried breathlessly.

"Oh my!" exclaimed Sir Lance. "Which of my knights will rid my kingdom of this awful creature?"

Sir Lance's knights were not too keen to take on the dragon.

"I think that Mr Uppity and his friends should deal with the menace seeing as they were so successful in the tournament," suggested the Yellow Knight.

Sir Lance agreed wholeheartedly.

Mr Uppity agreed halfheartedly.

The dragon was a truly fearsome and fiery beast.

Mr Uppity watched in horror as it burnt down
a house with one scorching breath.
"Any suggestions?" Mr Uppity asked, hopefully.

"How about the fire brigade?"
suggested Little Miss Greedy.

"Or Mr Strong?" remembered Mr Nosey.
"He's very good at putting out fires."

"Of course," cried Mr Strong. "Make way! I need a barn!"

Mr Strong rushed off and found an empty barn, he then filled the upside down barn with water from the moat and poured it over the dragon.

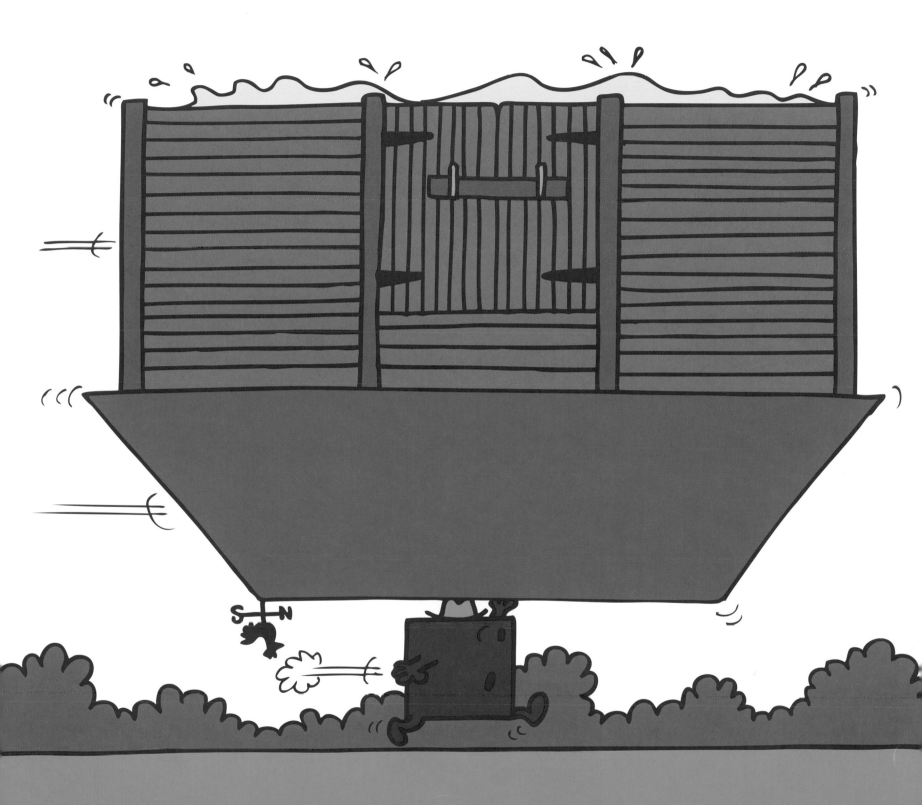

There was a loud hissing and sizzling sound.

The damp dragon tried to breath fire, but its fire was put out.

"Hurrah!" cried the crowd.

Sir Lance was so grateful that he offered Mr Uppity half his kingdom, but Mr Uppity explained that he was the richest man in the world and if he wanted half a kingdom he could buy it for himself.

"However," he said. "I would like to become a knight."

So Sir Lance knighted Mr Uppity.

"Arise Sir Uppity," he proclaimed.

It was one of the proudest moments of Mr Uppity's life.

And something that Mr Uppity did not let anyone forget.

Sorry ... Sir Uppity!